The Legend of

Jelly Bean

and the Unbreakable Egg™

Dear Reader—

When my son, Nicholas, was very young, our neighbor, who owned the farm next door, would invite all the children in Nick's school to come for an egg hunt. Dozens of children, hundreds of eggs, and acres of hiding places made for a wonderful long day of fun on the farm. The hunt was made even more exciting because our neighbor would also hide an unbreakable egg and the child who found that special egg won a basket of goodies. The unbreakable egg was actually a colorfully hand-painted egg-shaped rock. Nick found that egg one year and was more interested in how to open it than he was in the prize basket. That happy memory was the inspiration for the story you are about to read.

I wish you and everyone you make happy memories with all the best.

—Joe

For Barbara, my big sister, my best friend,
and a real good egg!

ISBN 978-0-545-53062-0

12 11 10 9 8 7 6 5 4 3   13 14 15 16 17 18/0

Printed in the U.S.A.   40

First Scholastic printing, March 2013

www.holidayhillfarm.com

The Legend of
Jelly Bean
and the Unbreakable Egg™

Written and created by Joe Troiano

Illustrated by Susan Banta

SCHOLASTIC INC.

It was just before Easter
on Holiday Hill Farm,
when five little chicks
hatched in back of the barn.

First came Rose.

Then came Violet.

Next Lily came along.

Then Daffodil and Tulip,
and then...

...something went wrong!

One little chick,
Chick Number Six,
couldn't get out of her egg—
the shell was too thick.

She tried every trick
that a chick knew to do.
She tried and she tried.
The others tried too.

They pecked it.
They poked it.
They gave it a whack!
But that unbreakable egg
just wouldn't crack.

So they begged,
and they pleaded.
They started to shout.
But that unbreakable egg
would not let her out.

Then the farmer came in
and took *Chick Six* away
with the rest of the batch
that hadn't hatched that day.

The chicks followed the farmer
past geese, goats, and cows,
up the front steps
and into his house.

There were eggs on the table.
There were eggs on the chairs.
There were dozens and dozens,
but which egg was theirs?

Then the five little chicks
heard a very soft rapping
and knew that *Chick Six*
was on the tabletop tapping.

The chicks flapped and they flapped
and they flew through the air.
They flew to the table,
but once they got there...

their wings were so tired,
their wings were so sore,
that the five little chicks
couldn't flap anymore.

One by one
the chicks dropped from the sky,
right into crocks
filled with Easter egg dye.

Now Rose was red,
and Violet was blue.
Lily was orange.
Tulip green through and through.
And Daffodil was as yellow
as any daffodil that grew.

Inside her egg, *Chick Six* started to cry.
The chicks followed the sound and found her nearby.

They attacked from the front.
They attacked from the back.
They attacked one by one.
They attacked in a pack.
But that unbreakable egg...still wouldn't crack.

So...they rolled it off the tabletop and watched it drop.

They were sure it would crack when it smacked on the floor, but it didn't...

it just bounced...

and bounced...

right out the front door.

The sun was setting and the barnyard was calm.
Mothers and babies were snuggling all over the farm.
The chicks realized, watching that egg roll along,
they had been going about this entirely wrong.

Instead of whacking,
and smacking,
and attacking that egg...

they should have been hugging,
and holding,
and hatching that egg.

So these birds of a feather all huddled together
to keep *Chick Six*, and her egg, nice and warm.

Then it started to drizzle, and the drops that fell
made the dye from their feathers drip onto the shell.
And the pattern the five different colors created
made that unbreakable egg look...decorated.

And on Easter morning,
with the sun shining bright,
the five little chicks
woke up from the night.

There were colorful pieces
of shell on the ground,
but where was *Chick Six*?
They looked all around.

Then out from the shadows stepped *Chick Number Six*,
and her feathers were a wonderful, colorful mix.
They were red, and blue, yellow, orange, and green.
So the chicks named *Chick Six*...JellyBean!

The chicks marched through the barnyard, proud as could be,
with JellyBean in front chirping, "Come on! Follow me!"

Every animal on the farm joined in the fun
and it was the best parade ever...the very best one.

You see...that egg wasn't unbreakable,
not one little bit.
The truth was...that egg didn't like to be hit.

So when you have a problem that grows and grows,
think of Daffodil, Tulip, Lily, Violet, and Rose.
And when you get stuck, and don't know what to do—

don't hit,
don't shout,
don't pout,
don't beg.

Remember,
there's more than one way
to crack an egg!